THREE WISHES

LUCILLE CLIFTON

THREE WISHES

Illustrated by Stephanie Douglas

THE VIKING PRESS NEW YORK

First Edition

Text copyright © 1974 by Lucille Clifton
Illustrations copyright © 1976 by Stephanie Douglas
All rights reserved
First published in 1976 by The Viking Press
625 Madison Avenue, New York, N.Y. 10022
Published simultaneously in Canada by
The Macmillan Company of Canada Limited
Printed in U.S.A.

1 2 3 4 5 80 79 78 77 76

Library of Congress Cataloging in Publication Data
Clifton, Lucille, 1936–   Three wishes.
Summary: When a young girl finds a good luck
penny and makes three wishes on it, she learns
that friendship is her most valued possession.
[1. Friendship—Fiction]   I. Douglas, Stephanie.
II. Title. PZ7.C6224Th   [E]   75-5579

ISBN 0-670-71063-6

To Rocky Ford and Tammy Fortune
Good Friends
L. C.

To Bweela, Javaka & Orin Sartha
Love
S. D.

Everybody knows there's such a thing as luck. Like when a good man be the first person to come in your house on the New Year Day you have a good year, but I know somethin better than that! Find a penny on the New Year Day with your birthday on it, and you can make three wishes on it and the wishes will come true! It happened to me.

First wish was when I found the penny. Me and Victorius Richardson was goin for a walk, wearin our new boots we got for Christmas and our new hat and scarf sets when I saw somethin all shiny in the snow.

Victor say, "What is that, Lena?"

"Look like some money," I say, and I picked it up. It was a penny with my birthday on it. 1962.

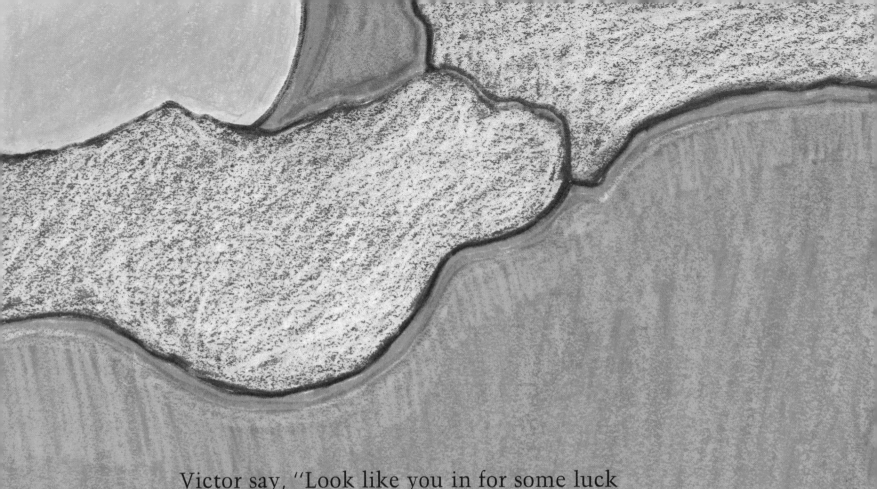

Victor say, "Look like you in for some luck now, Lena. That's a lucky penny for you. What you gonna wish?"

"Well, one thing I do wish is it wasn't so cold," I say just halfway jokin. And the sun come out. Just then.

Well, that got me thinkin. Me and Victor started back to my house both of us thinkin bout the penny and what if there really is such a thing and what to wish in case. Mama was right in the livin room when we got to the house.

"How was the walk, Nobie?"

"Fine thank you, Mama," I say.

"Fine thank you, ma'am," Victor say as we go back to the kitchen.

My name is Zenobia after somebody in the Bible. My name is Zenobia and everybody call me Nobie. Everybody but Victor. He call me Lena after Lena Horne and when I get grown I'm goin to Hollywood and sing in the movies and Victorius is gonna go with me cause he my best friend. That's his real name.

Back in the kitchen it was nice and warm cause the stove was lit and Mama had opened the oven door. Me and Victor at the table talkin soft so nobody can hear.

"You get two more wishes, Lena."

"You really think there's somethin to it?"

"What you mean, didn't you see how the sun come ridin out soon as you said about it bein too cold?"

"You really think so?"

"Man, don't you believe nothin?"

"I just don't believe everything like you do, that's all!"

"Well, you just simple!"

"Who you callin simple?"

"Simple you, that's who, simple Zenobia!"

I jumped up from the table. "Man, I wish you would get out of here!" and Victor

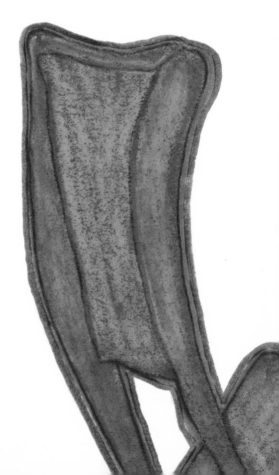

jumped up and ran out of the room and grabbed his coat and ran out of the house. Just then.

Well, I'm tellin you! I just sat back down at the table and shook my head. I had just about wasted another wish! I didn't have but one more left!

Mama come into the kitchen lookin for me. "Zenobia, what was the matter with Victorius?" She call me Zenobia when she kind of mad.

"We was just playin, Mama."

"Well, why did he run out of here like that?"

"I don't know Mama, that's how Victor is."

"Well, I hope you wasn't bein unfriendly to him Zenobia, cause I know how you are too."

"Yes, ma'am. Mama, what would you wish for if you could have anything you wanted in the whole wide world?"

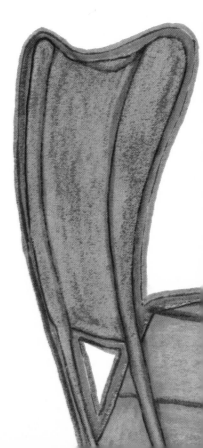

Mama sat down at the table and started playin with the salt shaker. "What you mean, Nobie?"

"I mean, if you could have yourself one wish, what would it be for?"

Mama put the salt back on a straight line with the pepper and got the look on her face like when she tellin me the old wise stuff.

"Good friends, Nobie. That's what we need in this world. Good friends." Then she went back to playin with the table.

Well, I didn't think she was gonna say that! Usually when I hear the grown people talkin bout different things they want, they be talkin bout money or a good car or somethin like that. Mama always do come up with a surprise!

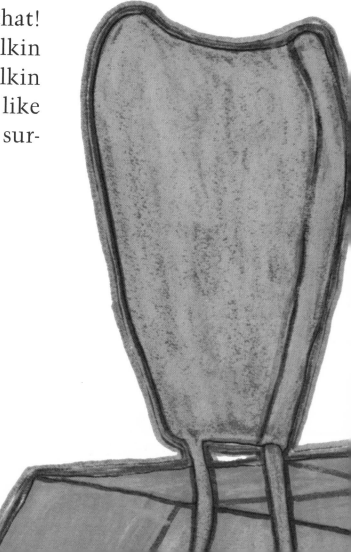

I got up and got my coat and went to sit out on the step. I started thinkin bout ole Victor and all the stuff me and him used to do. Goin to the movies and practicin my singin and playin touch ball and stick ball and one time we found a rock with a whole lotta shiny stuff in it look just like a diamond. One time me and him painted a picture of the whole school. He was really a good friend to me. Never told one of my secrets. Hard to find friends like that.

"Wish I still had a good friend," I whispered to myself, holdin the penny real tight and feelin all sorry for myself.

And who do you think come bustin down the street grinnin at me? Just then!

Yeah, there's such a thing as luck. Lot of people think they know different kinds of luck but this thing bout the penny is really real. I know cause just like I say, it happened to me.

ABOUT THE AUTHOR

LUCILLE CLIFTON was born in Depew, New York, and lived in Buffalo for most of her life. She attended Howard University in Washington, D.C., and is poet in residence at Coppin State College in Baltimore. Ms. Clifton has written numerous children's books, and her work has appeared in *Cricket, Mademoiselle, Ms., Black World,* and *The Atlantic.*

She and her husband and their six children live in Baltimore.

ABOUT THE ILLUSTRATOR

STEPHANIE DOUGLAS was born and grew up in New York City. She has illustrated another book by Lucille Clifton, *Good, Says Jerome.* The mother of three children, she and her family live in the Bronx, New York.

ABOUT THIS BOOK

The text type used in *Three Wishes* is Trump Medieval, and the display type face is Trump Gravur, set photographically. The full-color art work was done with pen and ink, crayon, and felt-tip markers, and the black-and-white art work was done with pen and ink and watercolor; both types of art were camera separated.